SOMEBODY STOLE SECOND

By Louise Munro Foley · Illustrated by John Heinly

A Yearling Book

Published by
Dell Publishing Co., Inc.
1 Dag Hammarskjold Plaza
New York, New York 10017

Yearling ® TM 913705, Dell Publishing Co., Inc.

ISBN:0-440-48126-0

Reprinted by arrangement with Delacorte Press.

Printed in the United States of America

Fourth Dell Printing—January 1978

*For Donald the Brave and
Billy, the Brave's little brother*

SOMEBODY STOLE SECOND

"It's GONE!" Pete yelled.
He stopped running.
Scooter stopped throwing.
And Jeff ran in from left field.

Pete was right.
It was gone.
Second base had disappeared.

"Fine thing," said Pete.
Pete was captain of the Jets.
"First time this year that I hit
a double . . . and when I get here,
second base is gone."

"Somebody stole second!" yelled Scooter
as he jumped up and down.
"Somebody stole second!"
He poked Pete in the ribs.
"Just like the Giants," yelled Scooter.
"Somebody stole second!"

"BE QUIET, SCOOTER!" yelled Pete.
"When the Giants steal second, it's GOOD.
THIS . . . IS BAD."

"Yeah," said Jeff, slowly. "Somebody
really stole second. They came along
and carted it away."

The three boys stared at the dirt
where second base used to be.
"Well, we still have first," said Jeff.
He was looking over at the orange towel
they used for first base.

"And THIRD!" yelled Scooter.
He ran down to check the
old piece of green carpet.

"But NO SECOND," said Pete.

Second base was an old red and black
car cushion. Or at least, it was
before it disappeared.

Pete's mother used to sit on it
when she was driving the car.

One day, Pete's father brought home
a new car cushion . . . so they put
the old cushion in Abner's
doghouse.

Abner was Pete's dog.
He was a funny dog.
He didn't like dog food.
He liked cherry vanilla ice cream.
He didn't like dog biscuits.
He liked graham crackers
(with butter and honey).

And he didn't like doghouses.
He liked Pete's bedroom.

So, when the Jets needed a second base,
Pete took Abner's red and black car cushion.

Abner never slept in the doghouse anyway.
He slept on a mat in Pete's bedroom until
Pete's mother turned out the light at night.

Every night, Pete's mother would
turn out the light and say . . .
"Good night, dear."

THEN . . .
Abner would jump into bed with Pete.
Pete had a nice soft bed with a
nice big pillow.

Pete would snuggle down beside Abner
and hug his pillow and go to sleep.

In the morning, Abner would jump out of
bed and lay down on the mat just before
Pete's mother came to wake them up.

So Abner didn't really need the doghouse . . .
or the car cushion.
He had Pete's bed to sleep in.

And that was how the car cushion
became second base.

Scooter sat down in the dirt.
"How can we play the Stars without a
second base?" he asked.

The Stars and the Jets were rivals.
They had a big game coming up the next
day It was a play-off.

"We can't," said Pete. "It's against
the rules to play without second base."

"We have to find it," said Jeff.
"Well, it didn't get up and walk away,"
said Scooter. "Somebody STOLE it."

"Hey!" yelled Jeff. "Who are our enemies?"

"The Stars!" yelled Pete.

"Girls!" yelled Scooter.

"BOTH!" yelled Jeff. "Let's go!"

The Jets went looking for the Stars.
The Stars were practicing for the big game.

"Keep your eyes open," whispered Pete.
"Maybe we'll spot it."

The Stars were good ball players.
They had four players.
They had two catcher's mitts.
And they had a second base.
But it wasn't the Jets' red and black
car cushion.
It was a dirty old potato sack.

"I don't see it," said Pete. "Let's go."

"Let's find Katy," said Jeff.
Katy was Jeff's sister. She was a pest.
And she was always playing tricks on the Jets.
One time, she stole their bats
and hid them in her doll buggy.
She even put doll clothes on the bats
to keep the boys from finding them.

They found Katy in Jeff's backyard.
"Somebody stole second base!" Scooter
yelled at Katy. "Did you steal second?"

Katy stuck out her tongue.
"Who'd want that dirty old red and black
cushion?" she said. "NOT ME!"

Jeff looked in her doll buggy.
He found two dolls, a half-eaten apple
and three of his new colored pencils.
But NO second base.

"She's not the crook," said Jeff.
"Let's go."

"Snack time," said Pete. "Let's get some cookies."
They went to Pete's house.
"Somebody stole second," Pete said to his mother.

"That's nice, dear," she said.

"THAT'S TERRIBLE!" yelled Pete.

"Don't yell, Peter," said Pete's mother.
She passed each of the boys two cookies.
"I thought baseball players always
stole second," she said.

"This wasn't a baseball player, Mom,"
said Pete, sadly. "This was a crook."

"I'm sorry," Pete's mother said.
She gave them each an extra cookie to
make them feel better.

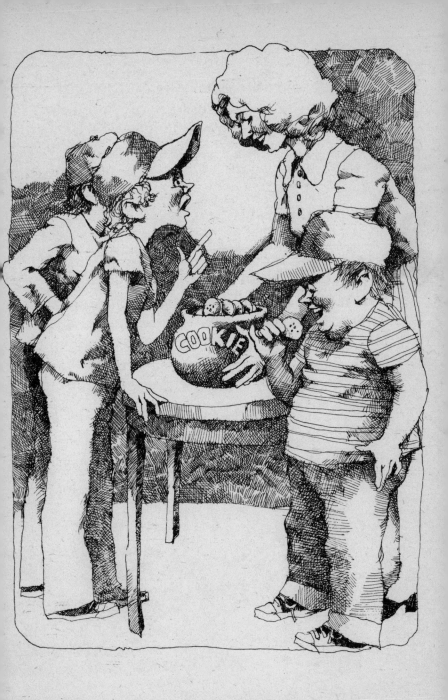

The boys spent all day looking for second base.
They asked a lot of people.
They asked a lot of kids.
They looked in a lot of funny places . . .
     the garage . . .
          the washing machine . . .
            the baby's sand box.

But they did not find second base.
They looked for a long time.
Then Pete had another idea.

"Maybe," he said, "just MAYBE . . .
Abner borrowed his pillow back."

32

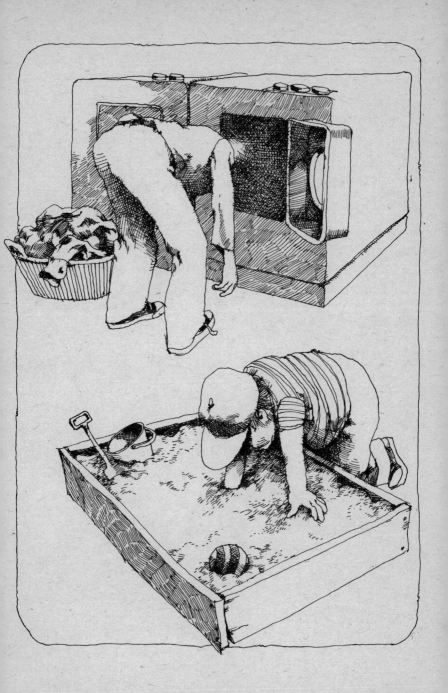

They ran out and looked in the doghouse.
It was dark inside.
Pete crawled in.
It was smelly.
"It's dark in here," he yelled.
His voice sounded funny.
He was holding his nose.
Scooter loaned him his flashlight.
"Nope!" Pete yelled. "No second base!"
He backed out of Abner's doghouse.

"No second base . . . no play-off tomorrow," said Scooter sadly.

"I'm tired of looking," said Jeff.

"Me, too," said Pete. "Let's go inside."

Pete's mother gave them a drink of milk.
Then they went upstairs to Pete's bedroom
to read.

Pete and Jeff flopped out on the floor.
Scooter flopped out on the bed.
He wiggled.
He squirmed.
He rolled over.
Then he looked at Pete and said,
"You have a lumpy bed."

"I have a nice bed!" yelled Pete, crossly.

"Lumpy!" yelled Scooter.
He pounded the bed with his fist.
"A great big lump, right here!"

Pete was mad. He got up to look.
Scooter was right.
His bed was lumpy.
"That's a new lump," said Pete.
"I've never seen that lump before."
He yanked down the bedspread.

"It's second base!" he yelled.
They all looked.
There it was . . . second base . . .
right in the middle of Pete's bed.

"ABNER DID IT!" yelled Pete. "Abner wanted a pillow! That dumb dog!"
He was laughing.
They were all laughing.
"This is going TOO far!" yelled Pete.

"He can eat my cherry vanilla ice cream . . .

and he can eat my graham crackers . . .

and he can sleep in my room . . .

BUT . . . he'll just have to find another pillow . . .

Because NOBODY . . . not even ABNER . . .
gets away with stealing second base
from the Jets!''

LOUISE MUNRO FOLEY lives in Sacramento, California, with her husband and two sons. She is the author of four books for young readers, and has written for radio and television. She is a native of Ontario, Canada.

JOHN HEINLY illustrated *The Strange Story of the Frog Who Became a Prince,* by Elinor Horwitz (Delacorte Press). The art director for the *Washington Evening Star*'s Sunday magazine supplement, he lives in Burke, Virginia, with his wife and son.